Health & Nutrition
Fitness

Health & Nutrition

Fitness

Food & Nutrition

Food Safety

Health & Hygiene

Healthy Diet

Malnutrition

Health & Nutrition

Fitness

MASON CREST
PHILADELPHIA
MIAMI

Mason Crest
450 Parkway Drive, Suite D
Broomall, Pennsylvania 19008
(866) MCP-BOOK (toll-free)
www.masoncrest.com

First printing
9 8 7 6 5 4 3 2 1

ISBN (series) 978-1-4222-4217-9
ISBN (hardback) 978-1-4222-4218-6
ISBN (ebook) 978-1-4222-7589-4

Cataloging-in-Publication Data on file with the Library of Congress

Developed and Produced by National Highlights Inc.
Interior and Cover Design: Jana Rade
Copy Editor: Adirondack Editing
Production: Michelle Luke

QR CODES AND LINKS TO THIRD-PARTY CONTENT

You may gain access to certain third-party content ("Third-Party Sites") by scanning and using the QR Codes that appear in this publication (the "QR Codes"). We do not operate or control in any respect any information, products, or services on such Third-Party Sites linked to by us via the QR Codes included in this publication, and we assume no responsibility for any materials you may access using the QR Codes. Your use of the QR Codes may be subject to terms, limitations, or restrictions set forth in the applicable terms of use or otherwise established by the owners of the Third-Party Sites. Our linking to such Third-Party Sites via the QR Codes does not imply an endorsement or sponsorship of such Third-Party Sites or the information, products, or services offered on or through the Third-Party Sites, nor does it imply an endorsement or sponsorship of this publication by the owners of such Third-Party Sites.

CONTENTS

KEY ICONS TO LOOK FOR

WORDS TO UNDERSTAND: These words with their easy-to-understand definitions will increase the reader's understanding of the text while building vocabulary skills.

SIDEBARS: This boxed material within the main text allows readers to build knowledge, gain insights, explore possibilities, and broaden their perspectives by weaving together additional information to provide realistic and holistic perspectives.

EDUCATIONAL VIDEOS: Readers can view videos by scanning our QR codes, providing them with additional educational content to supplement the text. Examples include news coverage, moments in history, speeches, iconic sports moments, and much more!

TEXT-DEPENDENT QUESTIONS: These questions send the reader back to the text for more careful attention to the evidence presented there.

RESEARCH PROJECTS: Readers are pointed toward areas of further inquiry connected to each chapter. Suggestions are provided for projects that encourage deeper research and analysis.

SERIES GLOSSARY OF KEY TERMS: This back-of-the-book glossary contains terminology used throughout this series. Words found here increase the reader's ability to read and comprehend higher-level books and articles in this field.

PHYSICAL FITNESS

Fitness is defined as being in shape or in good physical condition. A healthy diet and regular exercise are required to achieve great physical fitness and a state of well-being. Being fit is also necessary for being healthy. A fit person is more resistant to illnesses than an unfit person. A healthy level of physical and cardiovascular *fitness has a positive effect on emotional and mental well-being.*

WORDS TO UNDERSTAND

CARDIOVASCULAR: related to the heart and blood vessels

ENDURANCE: stamina

INFIRMITY: illness or weakness

HEALTH AND FITNESS

Health is a state of being free from any disease, stress, injury, pain, or illness. It's a combination of fitness and wellness—a truly healthy person not only feels good on the outside but also on the inside. According to the World Health Organization (WHO), "Health is a state of absolute physical, mental, and social well-being, and not just the absence of disease or infirmity." Although physical fitness and good health influence each other, they are not the same. Healthy people could also be physically unfit because of a lack of exercise. Physically fit people are able to perform their everyday tasks with ease.

MEASURE OF FITNESS

The level of physical fitness determines the kind of physical activity a person can perform, including the length of time and the level of intensity of that activity.

There are five overall measures of fitness:

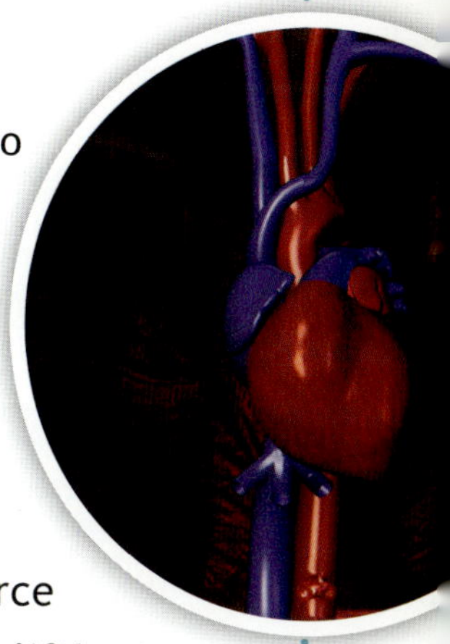

- **Cardiorespiratory endurance:** the heart's ability to pump strongly and efficiently, and of muscles to use oxygen more efficiently for longer periods of physical activity. To check your cardiorespiratory endurance, you can do a running test on a treadmill or any other flat surface.
- **Muscular strength:** the ability of muscles to exert force for a brief period. One can increase muscle strength by lifting weights and other such exercises.

- **Muscular endurance** is the ability of muscles to bear repeated contractions. Push-ups help to increase muscular endurance.
- **Body composition** refers to the amount of fat and muscle mass in the body. Since muscles weigh more than fat, it is important to measure body composition rather than body weight to check the fitness of a person. One of the easiest ways to measure body composition is through the **Body Mass Index** (BMI).
- **Flexibility** is the ability to move and use muscles freely. It's a good idea to practice stretching before and after each workout. Stretching is one of the easiest ways to assess the flexibility of each part of the body.

KEYS TO FITNESS

Drink plenty of water and exercise regularly to keep your body healthy and fit. Climbing stairs instead of using elevators or escalators and brisk walking are easy ways to maintain fitness.

DID YOU KNOW?

- The strongest muscle in the body is the masseter, located in the jaw.
- The heart is a vital muscle, and an average adult's heart beats more than one hundred thousand times a day.

MENTAL HEALTH

A healthy mind lives in a healthy body. A mentally sound person is sociable and resilient, meaning he or she is able to deal with stress and disappointment and with a positive attitude. Mentally healthy persons can make choices, be active, and feel confident. In short, mental health is about coping with the challenges of life, working productively and fruitfully.

WORDS TO UNDERSTAND

INTRUSIVE: unwelcome

RESILIENT: able to bounce back

SITUATIONAL: describes something that is caused by or is somehow related to particular circumstances

MENTAL ILLNESSES

Mental illnesses are medical conditions that affect a person's mood, behavior, and thinking. It is not always clear why some people develop mental illnesses while others do not. Genetics plays a role in some illnesses, while others are more situational in nature. Stress, exams, tension, poor nutrition, brain injury, family history, and trauma can alter specific parts of the brain and cause mental illnesses. Mental illnesses or mental disorders are divided into many types such as anxiety disorders (including obsessive-compulsive disorder and phobias), mood disorders (including depression and bipolar disorder), and psychotic disorders.

ANXIETY DISORDERS

Anxiety is an emotion that makes a person feel worried or nervous about something that is going to happen. All people feel anxiety from time to time—simply feeling anxious does not mean that someone has a disorder. People with an anxiety disorder feel worried with a frequency or to a degree that is not connected to their situation.

Obsessive-compulsive disorder (OCD) is a specific type of anxiety disorder in which people have intrusive and repeated thoughts, feelings, ideas, and sensations called obsessions. This makes a person perform repeated actions to make the thoughts or feelings go away. Repeated hand washing or repeatedly checking to make sure the front door is locked are examples of activities people with OCD may feel they have to perform.

PHOBIAS

A phobia is an anxiety disorder in which a person suffers from extreme fear of something. Fearing certain things helps a person avoid injuries or danger; excessive fear can lead to phobias. A phobia is a strong and unreasonable fear of something that causes little or no potential danger at all. Fear of heights, water, and the dark are some of the most common phobias.

MOOD DISORDERS

Mood disorders are mental health problems that affect how a person feels emotionally. Depression is one of the most common mood disorders. A person suffering from depression feels despaired, lonely, unhappy, and hopeless for a long time. It is perfectly normal to have these feelings from time to time, and if something bad happens in a person's life (such as the death of a loved one), that person might feel despair for some time. That doesn't mean the person has a mood disorder. Depression is a condition in which bad feelings continue and don't have any clear connection to the person's circumstances.

PSYCHOTIC DISORDERS

Psychotic disorders are severe mental illnesses in which a person suffers from abnormal thinking and perceptions. Schizophrenia is a lifelong psychotic disorder. People suffering from this disease hallucinate, see and hear things that are not there, and may feel that someone else is controlling their actions.

DID YOU KNOW?

- Mental illnesses are brain disorders. They aren't related to a person's intelligence or character and can't be overcome by willpower.
- Seasonal affective disorder (SAD) is a mood disorder that is triggered by the changing seasons of the year. It usually happens in the winter when there are fewer hours of sunlight.

Find out more about stress and how to deal with it.

DID YOU KNOW?

- Deep breathing can help reduce a person's stress and anger by focusing the mind.
- Taking B vitamins helps the brain maintain levels of the neurotransmitters dopamine and serotonin, which in turn can help with mood regulation.

OVERWEIGHT AND OBESITY

Being overweight means having body weight higher than what is standard for your height and bone structure. When one consumes more calories *than one can burn, the body stores the extra calories as fat. Hence, the energy imbalance between calories consumed and calories burned leads to the* accumulation *of body fat. Accumulation of body fat can result in the medical condition called obesity. Overweight and obese people are most likely to suffer from bone and joint problems, heart diseases, and sleep disorders.*

WORDS TO UNDERSTAND

ACCUMULATION: the amount of something that collects over time

BLOOD PRESSURE: the force with which blood flows from the heart throughout the body

CALORIE: a unit measuring how much energy one gets from food

SEDENTARY: describes someone who is not very active

OBESITY ON THE RISE

Obesity is on the rise globally. Almost one-third of people in the world meet the criteria for obesity. In the United States, one in three people are obese. There are many health risks associated with obesity. Heart disease, high blood pressure, and cancer are just a few of the health risks for an obese person. Of the top 10 causes of death in the world, the number one cause was heart disease—a problem that is not always caused by obesity but is very strongly associated with it.

WHAT CAUSES OBESITY?

The intake of more calories than the body burns leads to weight gain. The rise in the intake of energy-dense food that is high in salts and sugars, fried foods, and carbonated drinks are important causes of weight gain. These foods provide energy but lack vitamins, minerals, and other nutrients.

Another significant cause of overweight and obesity is lack of physical activity and a sedentary lifestyle. Improved modes of transportation and advanced technology have reduced the need for physical effort. Stress and anxiety, as well as some medical conditions, also cause people to gain extra weight.

LOSING WEIGHT

It takes a considerable amount of time for an obese person to lose weight. The results may be slow, but exercise does help. Aerobic exercises such as walking, jogging, swimming, weight training, and stretching exercises are all helpful. Water-related exercises are considered best for overweight and obese people, since water releases stress from the joints and does not cause much muscle fatigue. Even cycling on an exercise cycle at home or at a gym is helpful in reducing weight. Everyone should drink fluids before, during, and after exercise.

DID YOU KNOW?

- A bicycle rider participating in the Tour de France burns around 9,000 calories.
- Research suggests that those who exercise regularly are more productive at work.

HEALTHY BODY WEIGHT

A healthy body weight is one that is right for your particular height and build. It is the optimum weight at which a person feels fit, healthy, and energetic. Weight management is required to keep the body weight at a healthy level. Those with unhealthy weight are vulnerable to cardiovascular problems, diabetes, high blood pressure, as well as a weak immune system. On the other hand, people with ideal body weight are at a lower risk of health problems.

WORDS TO UNDERSTAND

CHOLESTEROL: a substance in the blood and cells of the body; too much cholesterol can cause heart disease

DIABETES: a medical condition in which the body does not produce enough insulin to reduce the amount of sugar in the blood

HORMONAL IMBALANCE: a medical condition in which someone has too much or too little of a particular hormone (a chemical substance that the cells, tissues, and organs use for communicating with each other)

PREDISPOSITION: natural inclination toward a certain thing

BMI CALCULATOR

You can measure your weight on a scale, but the scale doesn't take your height into account. For that reason, the better way to calculate weight is with the help of the Body Mass Index (BMI). The BMI is an estimate of the amount of body fat of a person. It is calculated by dividing a person's weight from his or her height.

Body Mass Index = Body Weight (pounds/kilograms)/ Height (feet/meters, squared)

Because the math can be a little tricky, the easiest way to calculate your BMI is to use one of the many calculators available online. The BMI indicates whether a person is underweight, overweight, obese, or a healthy weight. A BMI of 18.5 or below is an indicator that a person is underweight, whereas a BMI between 18.5 and 24.9 is considered healthy. A BMI that is greater than or equal to 25 is an indication of overweight. A BMI greater than or equal to 30 indicates obesity.

There are some limitations to the BMI. A very muscular person may have a higher BMI than you might expect—but that doesn't mean that the person is overweight. Additionally, BMI scales don't work very well for children and teens who are still growing. Physicians do calculate BMI for kids, but the BMI is considered in comparison to other kids of the same age. There are also separate BMI scales for males and females, because it's normal for the genders to have different amounts of body fat.

WEIGHT lbs	100	105	110	115	120	125	130	135	140	145	150	155	160	165	170	175	180	185	190	195	200	205	210	215
kgs	45.5	47.7	60.0	52.3	54.5	56.8	59.1	61.4	53.6	65.9	68.2	70.5	72.7	75.0	77.3	79.5	81.8	84.1	86.4	88.6	90.9	93.2	95.5	97.7
HEIGHT in/cm	Underweight					Healthy					Overweight					Obese				Extremely obese				
5'0" - 152.4	19	20	21	22	23	24	25	26	27	28	29	30	31	32	33	34	35	36	37	38	39	40	41	42
5'1" - 154.9	18	19	20	21	22	23	24	25	26	27	28	29	30	31	32	33	34	35	36	36	37	38	39	40
5'2" - 157.4	18	19	20	21	22	22	23	24	25	26	27	28	29	30	31	32	33	33	34	35	36	37	38	39
5'6" - 160.0	17	18	19	20	21	22	23	24	24	25	26	27	28	29	30	31	32	32	33	34	35	36	37	38
5'4" - 162.5	17	18	18	19	20	21	22	23	24	24	25	26	27	28	29	30	31	31	32	33	34	35	36	37
5'5" - 165.1	16	17	18	19	20	20	21	22	23	24	25	25	26	27	28	29	30	30	31	32	33	34	35	35
5'6" - 167.6	16	17	17	18	19	20	21	21	22	23	24	25	25	26	27	28	29	29	30	31	32	33	34	34
5'7" - 170.1	15	16	17	18	18	19	20	21	22	22	23	24	25	25	26	27	28	29	29	30	31	32	33	33
5'8" - 172.7	15	16	16	17	18	19	19	20	21	22	22	23	24	25	25	26	27	28	28	29	30	31	32	32
5'9" - 175.2	14	15	16	17	17	18	19	20	20	21	22	22	23	24	25	25	26	27	28	28	29	30	31	31
5'10" - 177.8	14	15	15	16	17	18	18	19	20	20	21	22	23	23	24	25	25	26	27	28	28	29	30	30
5'11" - 180.3	14	14	15	16	16	17	18	18	19	20	21	21	22	23	23	24	25	25	26	27	28	28	29	30
6'0" - 182.8	13	14	14	15	16	17	17	18	19	19	20	21	21	22	23	23	24	25	25	26	27	27	28	29
6'1" - 185.4	13	13	14	15	15	16	17	17	18	19	19	20	21	21	22	23	23	24	25	25	26	27	27	28
6'2" - 187.9	12	13	14	14	15	16	16	17	18	18	19	19	20	21	21	22	23	23	24	25	25	26	27	27
6'3" - 190.5	12	13	13	14	15	15	16	16	17	18	18	19	20	20	21	21	22	23	23	24	25	25	26	26
6'4" - 193.0	12	12	16	14	14	15	15	16	17	17	18	18	19	20	20	21	22	22	23	23	24	25	25	26

WEIGHT AND HEALTH PROBLEMS

Unhealthy weight causes many health-related illnesses. The additional weight affects a person's joints, backbone, breathing pattern, sleep, mood, behavior, and energy levels. It puts stress on joints, especially the hips and knees. The bones and muscles of the backbone also feel strained. Unhealthy body weight raises blood pressure and blood cholesterol levels, and increases the chances of developing diabetes and heart diseases.

WEIGHT CONTROL

Exercise regularly and avoid sitting in the same place for too long. Participate in outdoor activities, such as soccer, rather than watching TV, playing video games, or sitting at the computer. Eat a balanced diet that includes lots of fresh fruits and vegetables. Do not overeat, and avoid junk food, which has a lot of sugar, fat, and salt. Also, get plenty of sleep.

UNDERWEIGHT

Underweight means weighing less than what is considered healthy. Some people may have difficulty gaining weight due to a genetic predisposition, hormonal imbalances, or some other health issues. An underweight person is at a greater risk of suffering from bone loss and a weakened immune system, which can make the person more susceptible to infections.

DID YOU KNOW?

- The BMI was invented by Adolphe Jacques Quetelet.
- Obesity is one cause of sleep apnea—a medical condition in which a person suffers from pauses in breathing.

GOOD SLEEP: THE KEY TO FITNESS

Sleep is the state of complete inactivity of voluntary muscles and reduced sensory activity. It helps in the growth and **rejuvenation** *of the immune, nervous, skeletal, and muscular systems. It slows down the metabolism of the body and conserves energy. Sleep affects a person's mental and physical health. It also affects the normal functioning of the body. Our body requires sleep as much as it requires food, water, and air for survival.*

WORDS TO UNDERSTAND

LONGEVITY: to live a long and healthy life

PARALYZED: a condition in which the body becomes incapable of movement

REJUVENATION: to feel energetic and fresh

SLEEP CYCLE

The sleep cycle usually repeats four or five times throughout the night. One sleep cycle lasts about 90 to 100 minutes.

Stage 1: Drowsiness

In the initial stage, the brain sends a signal to the body to relax. The person's heart rate and breathing begin to slow down.

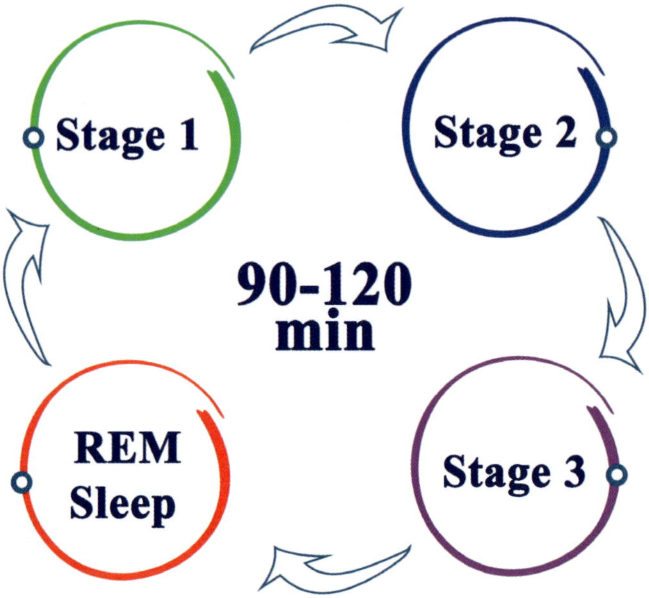

Stage 2: Light Sleep

A person falls asleep but has not progressed to deep sleep. The muscle activities slow down and a slight twitching may occur. This is the period of light sleep, which means a person can be awakened easily at this stage.

Stage 3: True Sleep

In this stage, our sleep is deep and restful. Brain activity along with breathing and heart rate become slower. True sleep is the longest stage of the sleep cycle. If a person is awakened at this stage, he or she will feel irritated or groggy for several minutes after waking up.

Stage 4: Deep Sleep/REM Sleep

This is the last stage of the sleep cycle. The eyes move under the eyelids, which is called Rapid Eye Movement (REM). This is the stage at which dreaming takes place and the brain becomes very active. Breathing and heart rate become very irregular and the body becomes paralyzed so it is not possible to act out one's dreams. After the last stage, the sleep cycle returns to light sleep and the cycle repeats.

SLEEP WELL

Try to schedule your sleeping hours and stick to them, even on weekends or holidays. Following a sleep schedule will habituate the body to the sleep-wake cycle and encourages sound sleep. When your bedtime approaches, do things to help yourself begin to relax, such as taking a shower, reading a book, or listening to music.Such relaxing activities provide a smooth transition from wakefulness to drowsiness. Make sure the bedroom is noise-free and dark. Try to avoid having big meals, or drinking soda or coffee just before going to bed. Avoid taking longer daytime naps and limit their span to 10 to 30 minutes, especially during the afternoon.

IMPORTANCE OF SLEEP

The brain needs sleep so that the power of memory can be preserved. Without enough sleep, a person finds it hard to focus, pay attention, or respond quickly. Lack of sleep also causes fatigue and sleepiness, leading to mood swings. Research has suggested that lack of sleep can even cause weight gain: overtired people are more likely to eat more than those who are well rested. That's because when

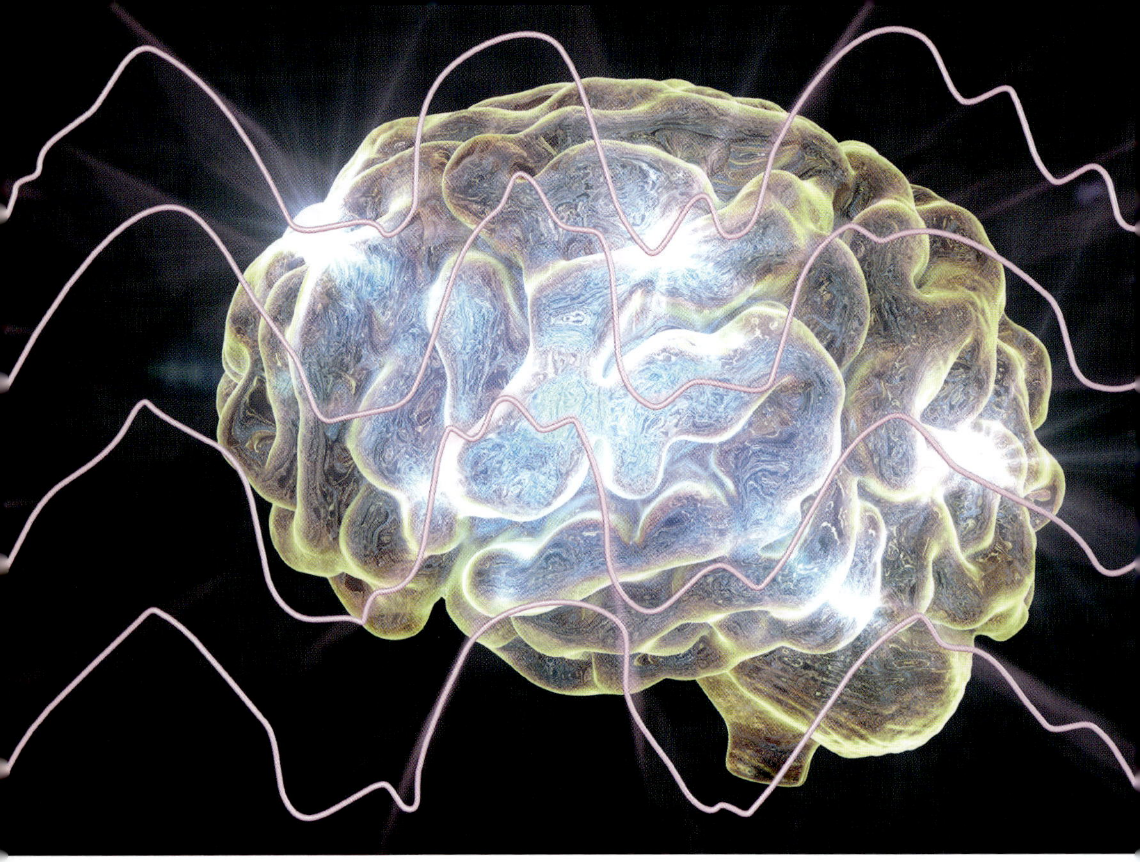

the body feels tired, it sends signals that some energy is needed, and sometimes that gets misinterpreted as hunger.

A good night's sleep improves memory and helps people to perform well in their daily tasks. During sleep, the body repairs itself. Our body cells produce more protein during sleep. The protein helps in repairing damaged cells. It also reduces stress, keeps the heart healthy, and promotes physical health, **longevity,** and emotional well-being.

DID YOU KNOW?

- An average human being spends one-third of his or her life asleep.
- The difference between the hours of sleep you need and the hours you actually get is called sleep debt.

SLEEP DEPRIVATION

Lack of sleep can lead to sleep deprivation, which can take a toll on one's health. Difficulties in falling asleep, rising too early in the morning, or feeling drowsy during the day are all possible signs of sleep disorders. Sleep disorders disturb the functions of the brain and can affect the overall well-being of a person. Some common sleep disorders are insomnia, sleep apnea, narcolepsy, and **restless leg syndrome**. *Sleep disorders have negative effects on one's physical, mental, and emotional health.*

WORDS TO UNDERSTAND

CHRONIC: a serious illness or pain that lasts for a long time

NIGHT TERROR: a sleep disorder in which a person quickly wakes from sleep in a frightened state

RESTLESS LEG SYNDROME: a sleep disorder in a person who suffers from an urge to move the legs to avoid unpleasant sensations

COMMON CAUSES

Stress and anxiety are two of the most common causes of sleep disorders. In today's competitive world, almost everybody suffers from stress and anxiety. However, when stress begins to take a toll on one's health, it is time to take it seriously. Mood disorders such as depression and other medical conditions can also cause trouble sleeping. Daily routines such as drinking too much caffeine, watching too much TV at night, or working late can disrupt one's sleep routine.

COMMON SYMPTOMS

Not being able to sleep even after going to bed, or waking up frequently in the night and

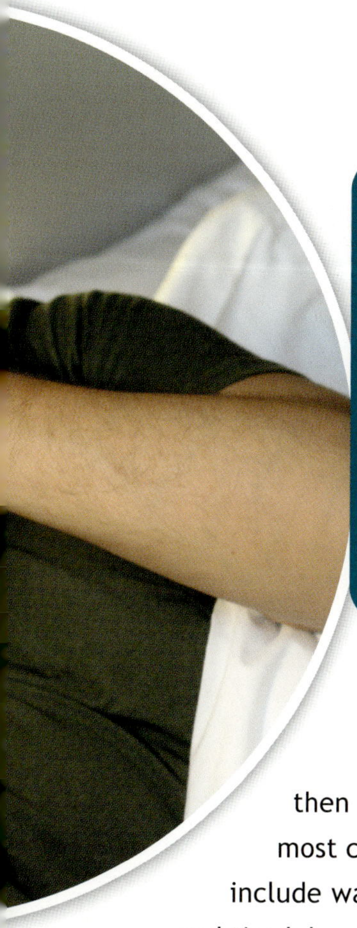

Here's some more information about the importance of sleep.

then having difficulty falling back to sleep are two of the most common symptoms of sleep disorders. Other symptoms include waking up very early in the morning or feeling irritated and tired despite sleeping for seven to eight hours. If you feel sleepy during the day and nap whenever possible or fall asleep at inappropriate times during the day, you are suffering from a sleep disorder. Sleep disorders make it difficult to concentrate and remember things.

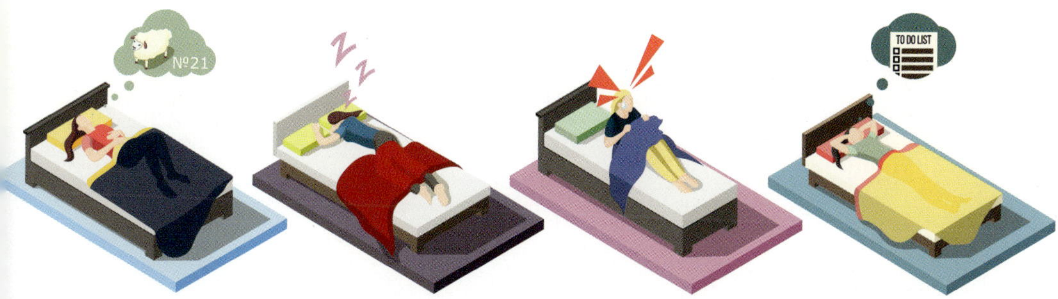

SLEEP APNEA

In this sleep disorder, breathing stops briefly during sleep due to blockage of the upper airways. This causes pauses in sleep, awakening one too many times, thus disrupting sleep. Sleep apnea can be potentially life threatening if not treated. Loud snoring is a common symptom of sleep apnea.

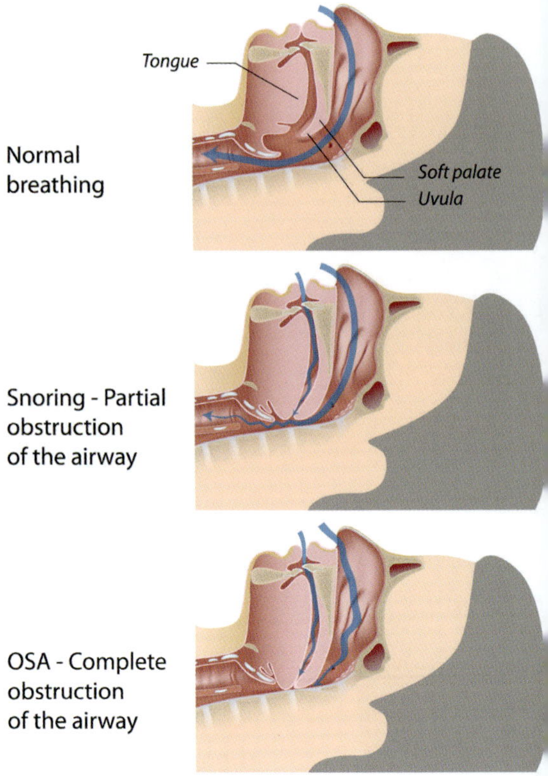

INSOMNIA

Insomnia is the most common sleep disorder. An insomniac cannot fall asleep easily and has trouble staying asleep for a long period. As a result, the person does not get enough sleep to wake up feeling refreshed and rested.

NARCOLEPSY

A person suffering from narcolepsy experiences excessive sleepiness during the day. This causes severe drowsiness followed by a sleep attack. Sleep attacks can occur anytime—while working, studying, or driving or during a class.

DID YOU KNOW?

- According to research by the National Commission on Sleep Disorders, 40 million people in the United States suffer from chronic sleep disorders.
- Sleepwalking and night terrors are two common sleep disorders.

EVERYDAY ACTIVITIES

An easy way to stay fit is to participate in daily activities that require physical effort. Everyday activities such as gardening, walking, playing with your pet, taking the stairs, and even working in the kitchen are all different forms of exercise. These activities help to burn fat and **facilitate** *weight management.*

Even household chores burn calories. Chores such as vacuuming, mopping, sweeping, and dusting are easy-to-do physical activities. More energy-consuming chores such as decorating the house, cleaning the refrigerator, spring cleaning, and the like are strenuous workouts. Polishing, dusting, mopping, and sweeping are great for keeping arms in shape. Bending and stretching when you make the bed, wash windows, or do the laundry are good for toning thighs and improving flexibility.

WORDS TO UNDERSTAND

EXERTION: effort

FACILITATE: to make easier

WEEDING: the process of removing weeds or unwanted plants from a garden

GARDENING: DIG THE BENEFITS

Gardening involves different types of exercises such as stretching, lifting weight, and a little cardiovascular workout. These exercises help in lowering blood pressure and cholesterol levels, and are good for the heart and for weight management. Raking, digging, planting saplings, mowing the lawn, weeding, pruning, and watering plants are some of the physical activities performed during gardening. It helps to tone the joints and the muscles of arms, legs, back, and abdomen. Pruning trees and shrubs is equal to walking at a normal pace.

CAR WASHING

Car washing involves a good amount of physical effort. Instead of taking the car to the car wash and letting a machine clean it, pull out the hose and grab a scrubber to begin washing. It involves bending, stretching, squatting, and moving the hands in a circular motion. This strengthens the muscles and joints of the shoulders, neck, arms, back, abdomen, and legs. Standing on the toes to clean the top of the car is a great workout for calf muscles and toes. According to a study, washing and waxing a car for about 39 minutes can burn about 275 calories.

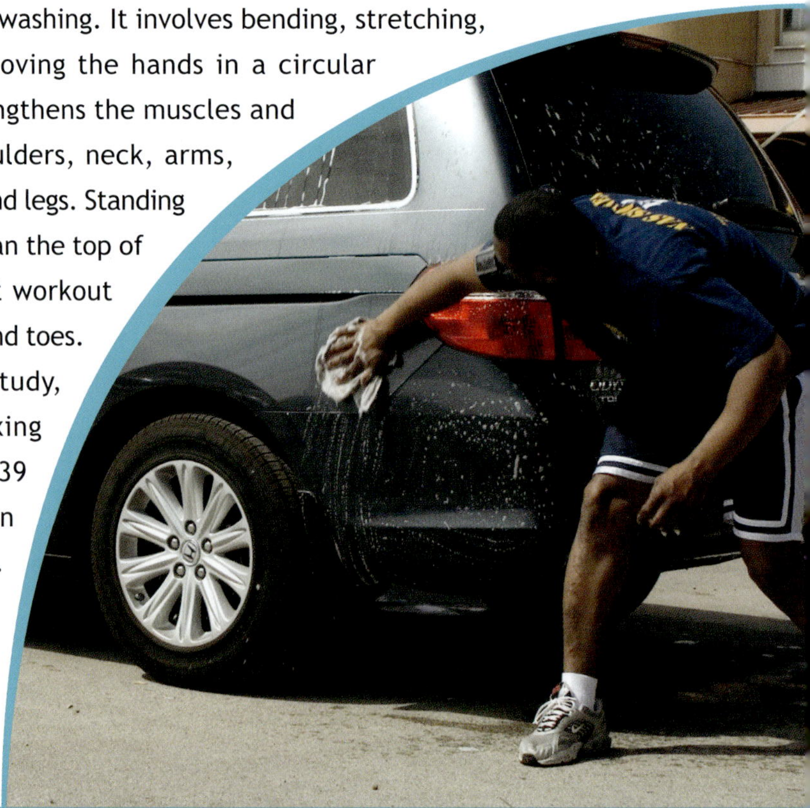

VACUUMING

Vacuuming helps strengthen the arms. In fact, it involves a workout of the entire body. To give both arms a better workout, try switching arms while vacuuming. Maintaining a correct posture when you vacuum also helps in strengthening the abdominal muscles. According to a study, vacuuming for 30 minutes burns about 90 calories.

MOPPING

Mopping the bathroom or the kitchen floor helps in strengthening and toning shoulders and biceps. Many researchers have noted that mopping the floor for merely 30 minutes burns about 112 calories. To give the body a more efficient workout, scrub the floor by getting down on your hands and knees. Scrubbing with a sponge or brush burns about 200 calories in 30 minutes. For better results, begin by scrubbing the dirtiest areas and then move on to cleaner areas.

COOKING

Many people think that cooking does not involve much physical activity. However, that's not completely true. Cooking may not involve a strenuous workout, but around one hour spent in the kitchen can help burn approximately 150 calories. On cooking shows, the chefs walk about the cooking space, bend, move their hands and neck, and do many other light exercises. These activities engage the muscles of our body.

WASHING DISHES

Scrubbing the dishes by hand instead of putting them in the dishwasher will burn approximately 160 calories in 30 minutes. Loading the dishwasher, on the other hand, burns about 105 calories in the same amount of time. Therefore, if time permits, you should try to scrub the dishes. It will be a light workout for the arm muscles and the upper body.

LAUNDRY

Putting the laundry away, lifting the laundry basket, hanging clothes outside on a clothesline, and picking up dry clothes are some physical activities that strengthen the arms, hands, upper back, and abdominal muscles. Even folding laundry is a good workout. Folding clothes for only 30 minutes can burn about 72 calories.

GROCERY SHOPPING

Going grocery shopping helps build strength and endurance since it requires a good deal of physical stamina. Pushing a shopping cart up and down the aisles is a good workout. Bagging the groceries, loading them in the car, returning the shopping cart to its place, carrying the groceries into the house, and putting them away are some activities that keep a person physically active. Shopping for groceries helps with weight control as it burns calories.

CLIMBING STAIRS

Every time you climb the stairs instead of taking the elevator, you are burning extra calories. It also helps to build muscles and increases your strength and endurance. Take the stairs whenever possible; in fact, try to make it a part of your daily routine.

WALKING

Walking is one of the easiest forms of exercise. Even though it's not a lot of exertion, a good amount of walking can still improve the health of our heart. If it is difficult to make time to go for walks, walk your pets. Extend the duration of the walk by 10 to 15 minutes to build stamina. Even playing with your pet is a good workout. Playing fetch is known to burn about 115 calories per hour.

DANCING

Dancing is a great workout for the mind and body. It requires the dancer to remember the steps, which helps in boosting memory skills. Dancing is a fitness activity that is good for people of all ages. It builds up bones and muscles, improves posture and balance, and increases stamina and flexibility.

DID YOU KNOW?

- Household chores can help a person burn 50,000 calories a year.
- Raking leaves is a type of weight training due to the resistance offered by the leaves. Doing it for 30 minutes helps burn 225 calories.

AEROBIC EXERCISES

Aerobic exercises enhance endurance and strengthen the heart and lungs by making them move in rhythmic and continuous motion.

These are also known as cardiovascular exercises. They involve physical activity of moderate intensity and are performed for extended periods. Walking, running, cycling, hiking, and swimming are the different types of aerobic exercises.

WORDS TO UNDERSTAND

AEROBIC: exercise that improves the body's ability to absorb oxygen and move it around the body

CARDIORESPIRATORY: related to the functions of both heart and lungs

METABOLISM: the process in which cells produce energy and other substances necessary for life from the food that a person eats

WALKING

Walking is the easiest way to exercise, as no special equipment is needed. You should walk for at least 30 minutes every day. This improves the lower body muscles as well as cardiovascular fitness. Walking is a weight-bearing activity and thus helps in improving bone density. It also puts less stress on the joints as compared to the other exercises.

RUNNING

Running is another easy and very effective way to stay fit. All it requires is a good pair of sports shoes, and you are all set! Running and jogging are roughly the same, although people usually describe jogging as running at a slow pace. Running increases cardiorespiratory fitness and bone density. It also reduces sleep disorders and burns calories. It is advisable to not start running in the first few days; start by walking briskly and then jogging slowly. Running can be tough on the knees, however.

SWIMMING

Swimming is an excellent exercise. A swimmer needs to swim against the resistance of water, which requires a lot of physical effort. It involves the movement of all the muscles and joints, and it improves cardiovascular health. Swimming also increases blood circulation and lung capacity. Water supports body weight, so swimming does not put stress on the joints the way running can.

CYCLING

Cycling is one of the most enjoyable and result-oriented sports. Cycling involves the largest muscle groups of the body, especially the legs. It strengthens leg muscles and the mobility of the hip and knee joints. Cycling helps build muscles and improves stamina and fitness. It is also a good way to improve cardiovascular fitness since the heart pounds in a stable manner during cycling. Regular cycling can increase cardiovascular fitness by 3–7 percent. It also increases the body's metabolism after the ride has been finished.

HIKING

Popular as one of the healthiest aerobic sports, hiking is an exercise of moderate intensity. The health benefits of hiking are enormous. A great deal of muscle movement is involved in hiking, which helps to build muscle strength. It also improves stamina and promotes weight loss. Along with other aerobic exercise, hiking helps one develop resistance to health risks, such as obesity, heart disease, high blood pressure, type 2 diabetes, stroke, and certain types of cancer.

DID YOU KNOW?

- Freestyle swimming can burn 100 calories every 10 minutes.
- Cycling at a steady pace can burn approximately 300 calories per hour.

ANAEROBIC EXERCISES AND SPORTS

Anaerobic means "without oxygen." Weightlifting, push-ups, pull-ups, rowing, and jumping rope are some anaerobic physical activities. They do more for muscle strength than for the cardiovascular system.

Playing sports is an enjoyable way to improve the levels of fitness and to manage weight. They can be performed for longer durations than anaerobic exercises can. Both anaerobic exercises and sports help to build muscles and to enhance muscle size and strength.

WORDS TO UNDERSTAND

ANAEROBIC: describes exercises that are not intended to improve the cardiovascular system

COORDINATION: the ability of different body parts to work together well

MOBILITY: the ability of something to move well

WEIGHTLIFTING

Weightlifting helps make bones and muscles stronger and is an effective workout for burning fat. Unlike other forms of exercises that burn fat only while working out, weightlifting keeps the calories burning long after the workout is over. Muscle tissues stoke the metabolic rate and cause one to burn more calories per hour. Weightlifting enhances coordination and stamina, and improves the mobility of joints.

BASKETBALL

Basketball is a team sport in which players have to throw a ball through a basket. The game includes running, jumping, dribbling, shooting, passing, and rebounding. It is a good workout to build muscle endurance and strength, improve coordination and balance, and help in developing concentration and confidence. Playing this sport is known to burn around 630–750 calories per hour.

GOLF

Golf is played outdoors in vast green surroundings. In this sport, a player has to strike the golf ball into a series of holes with as few strokes as possible using a golf club. It requires a player to walk a lot, carrying or pulling golf clubs. On average, a golf player can walk up to four miles on a golf course. This sport provides a good cardiovascular workout, building muscle endurance and strength.

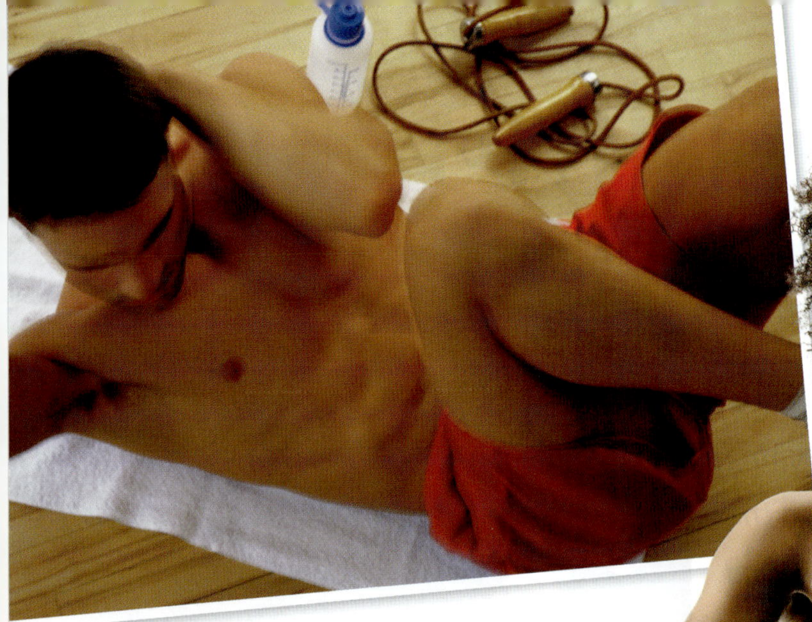

BENEFITS OF STRETCHING

The biggest benefit of stretching is that it enhances the flexibility of the body. Lack of flexibility not only slows down our movement, it also makes us vulnerable to muscle strains and soft-tissue injuries. Stretching helps in maintaining body balance and coordination by improving flexibility. It also improves blood circulation in the body, promotes cardiovascular health, and eases stiffness or tightness in the lower back, hamstrings, and buttocks.

STATIC STRETCHING

In static stretching, the body is in a state of rest even as the muscles are stretched. It is also known as "low-load prolonged stretch." This type of stretching can be done following various techniques that stretch the muscle to an elongated position. It is important to hold the position for at least 30 seconds. One may feel a warm sensation in the muscles, which is normal and not an indicator of any kind of injury. However, it is best to avoid static stretching before playing sports such as soccer, rugby, and others.

DYNAMIC STRETCHING

Dynamic stretching is the most commonly recommended warm-up exercise. In this type of stretching, the body is in motion while simultaneously doing a series of muscle stretches. Also, you don't need to hold the end position while doing dynamic stretching. It increases blood circulation in the muscle area and warms up the body for a strenuous sport session ahead.

Check out this video with basic stretching exercises.

STRETCHING GUIDELINES

- Never hold your breath while stretching.
- Stretching should not cause any pain. If there is any such occurrence, it indicates that the muscles are not being stretched in the right way.
- Never bounce while stretching.

Stretching Before Workout

- relaxes muscles
- increase flexibility and movement
- corrects exercise posture
- provides coordination

Stretching After Workout

- relaxes muscles
- slows down heartbeat to a normal speed
- returns breathing to its normal pace
- reduces stiffness and soreness of the muscles

DID YOU KNOW?

- Exercising triggers the brain to release endorphins.
- People lose muscle mass as they age.

SPORTS AND EXERCISE INJURIES

There is always a risk of injury in any type of physical activity, but the benefits of physical activities usually outweigh the risks. Sports- and exercise-related injuries can be prevented and their risk can be reduced with proper preparation and quality equipment. Some of the most common exercise-related injuries are muscle **sprain** *and strain, muscle spasms and cramps,* **tendinitis***, bruises, overuse injuries, and others.*

WORDS TO UNDERSTAND

AILMENT: illness or condition

SPRAIN: to wrench or twist a joint or muscle

TENDINITIS: a condition where a tendon becomes inflamed, usually from overuse

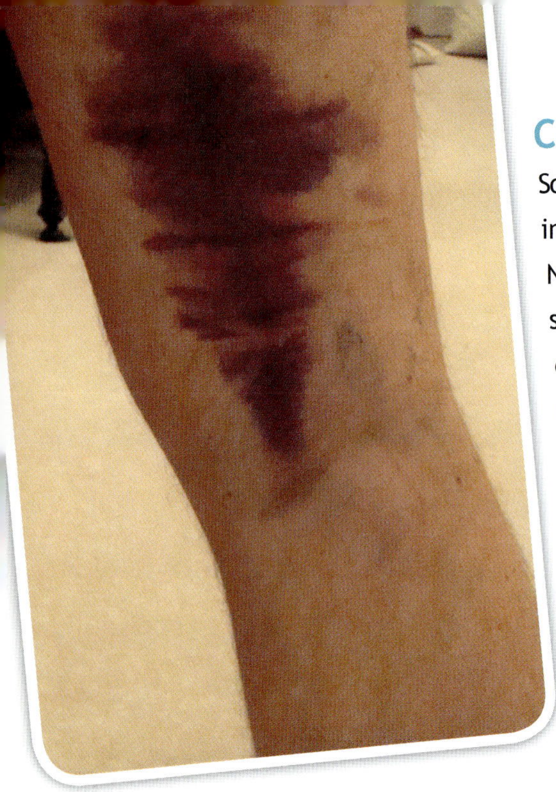

CAUSES OF INJURIES

Some of the most common causes of exercise-related injuries are poor technique and inexperience. Not using the right equipment while exercising, such as shoes, clothes, helmet, and the like can expose you to injuries. Increasing the duration and intensity of exercise too soon can also take a toll on health. Exercising outdoors in extremely hot or cold weather without proper fitness equipment increases the chances of injuries. If a person has been injured in the past or suffers from other medical ailments, the risk of exercise-related injuries is always higher.

TISSUE INJURIES

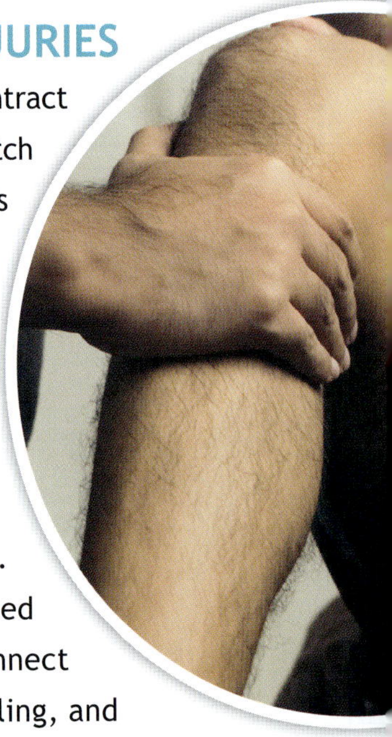

Muscles and tendons are composed of tissues that can contract and stretch. If sudden force is applied, the tissues stretch beyond their capacity, which may cause the blood vessels to rupture. Ruptured blood vessels lead to swelling of the particular area. It can take a few weeks to recover; specific recovery time depends on the seriousness of the particular injury.

COMMON INJURIES

Tendons are tissues that connect muscles to the joints. Strain occurs when muscles or tendons are overstretched or torn. Muscle sprain occurs when ligaments that connect joints and support them are overstretched. Pain, swelling, and stiffness are a few symptoms of muscle strain and sprain. The soreness of tendons causes tendinitis, leading to pain, swelling, and redness. Muscle cramps and spasms are the result of strong muscle contractions. Other than these, there are overuse injuries caused by repetitive stress on and motion of body parts, such as muscles, tendons, joints, bones, and nerves.

RISK REDUCTION

Warm-up activities help the body to prepare for a workout session. On the other hand, cooling down after exercise relaxes the body and reduces stress from the muscles and joints. Stretching must be done before and after exercise. Use appropriate fitness equipment that is in good working condition. Learn the right technique and body posture to avoid injuries. Consult a fitness instructor or coach to know what kind of exercises or fitness activities suit you. Increase the duration and intensity of the exercise over time.

DID YOU KNOW?

- Bruises are injuries in which bleeding occurs under the skin. This type of bleeding makes the bruise look bluish.
- Do gentle stretches and drink plenty of fluids to ease muscle cramps.

EXERCISE SAFETY

Physical exercise is one of the best ways to stay fit and maintain a healthy weight. You can effectively reduce various health risks by exercising for only 30 minutes, three to five times a week. Although exercise is good for health, it can also cause damage to the body when not done in the right way with the right equipment. Therefore, exercise safety is of utmost importance.

WORDS TO UNDERSTAND

REGIMEN: a clear plan to follow, such as a diet or exercise plan

TREADMILL: a machine that allows a person to walk or run in place

VIGOROUS: energetic

LISTEN TO YOUR BODY

Go for a regular medical checkup before starting out on a fitness regimen. Take a break from the exercise routine if there is fatigue or body ache. Usually, people try to train themselves too hard or too fast, which increases the chances of injury. Torn or sprained muscles and ligaments are some common exercise injuries. In case an injury occurs, you should take a break and avoid exercising.

A SLOW START

To begin a regular exercise routine, start slowly. One needs to build stamina and accustom the body to physical exertion. Most exercise-related injuries occur when a beginner pushes too hard. You should begin with only 10 minutes of exercise (push-ups, jogging, running, or swimming). Gradually increase the duration and intensity of the exercise.

CHOOSE THE RIGHT EQUIPMENT

Shoes, helmets, goggles, and treadmills are all exercise equipment. Make sure to use durable and good-quality exercise equipment. Get the right pair of shoes according to the type of physical activity; for example, you may need a pair of shoes with excellent arch support and a tread that works on different surfaces for running. A tennis player needs shoes with good ankle support and flat tread.

LEARN THE RIGHT TECHNIQUE

You should make sure that the exercises are being performed in the right manner. Holding wrong positions while exercising can cause serious injuries. A fitness enthusiast should learn all the proper exercise techniques. If possible, seek the help of a professional trainer.

ELLIPTICAL TRAINER

An elliptical trainer is also known as a cross-trainer. It helps the user imitate the actions of climbing stairs, walking, or running. It's useful because using the trainer puts less pressure on the joints than, for example, running on a flat road. It also lets the user exercise the upper body through the back-and-forth movements of arms and the lower body through the movement of legs.

EXERCISE BALL

An exercise ball is one of the most commonly used pieces of fitness equipment. It is made of an elastic material and is filled with air. It is used for stretching, bending, and as a training aid in a number of exercises. It introduces instability to an exercise that would not be there normally, thus forcing the body to maintain balance. An exercise ball is mostly used for building and strengthening the core muscles of the body, especially the abdominal and back muscles. It is also known as a Swiss ball, fitness ball, gym ball or balance ball.

FREE WEIGHTS

Barbells, dumbbells, kettlebells, and medicine balls are different types of weights. Weights are used to build and tone arm muscles and strengthen arms and hands. A barbell is a large bar with weights on both ends. It is gripped by both hands and is lifted up to the shoulders for rest. On the other hand, a dumbbell is a small bar with weight on both ends that can be held in one hand.

DID YOU KNOW?

- Aquilino Cosani, an Italian plastics manufacturer, developed the first Swiss ball or exercise ball in 1963.
- Many gyms also organize aerobic dance and kickboxing classes.

GOOD POSTURE

The way a person sits, stands, walks, sleeps, and holds his or her body is called posture*. Good posture means training the body to stand, sit, sleep, or walk in a way that puts less strain on supporting muscles and joints during movement and lifting weights. It is also believed that correct posture not only keeps the mind calm and relaxed but also helps one to maintain physical stability.*

WORDS TO UNDERSTAND

LUMBAR ROLL: a cylindrical cushion that provides support and comfort to the lower back

MUSCULOSKELETAL: the muscular and skeletal system of the body

POSTURE: the way a person holds up his or her body

IMPORTANCE OF GOOD POSTURE

Body posture has long-term effects on the musculoskeletal system. In the correct posture, the body parts are aligned perfectly and the muscles and joints work in accordance. This decreases the abnormal wearing of joint surfaces, which can cause joint pain or arthritis. The muscles work efficiently, thereby allowing the body to use less energy. A good posture also reduces backache and muscular pain.

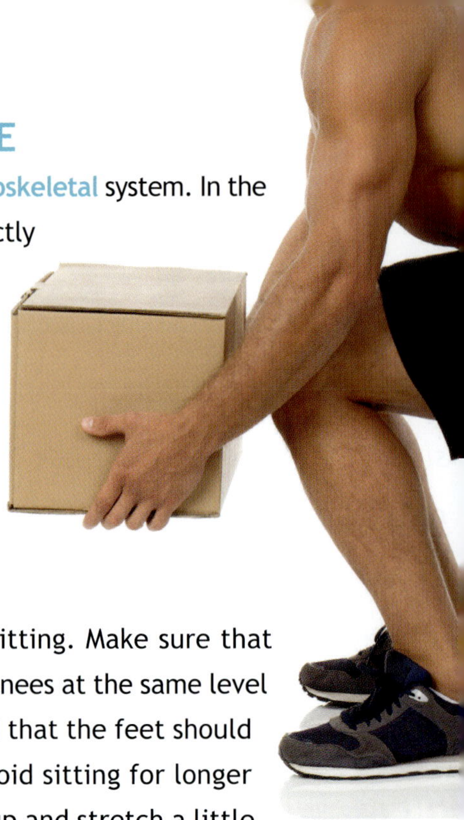

SITTING POSTURE

Keep your back and shoulders straight while sitting. Make sure that your hips touch the back of the chair. Keep the knees at the same level or a little higher up than the hips. Bear in mind that the feet should touch the floor. Do not cross your legs, and avoid sitting for longer than 30 minutes at a time. Take breaks to get up and stretch a little.

LIFTING POSTURE

To lift an object, keep the back straight and bend the knees and hips. Avoid bending forward from the waist with the knees straight. Keep the feet firmly on the ground, grab the object, and lift it by straightening the legs while standing up. Avoid pulling the object with sudden force, and hold it close to the body. Remember to move the feet forward when lifting an object.

POOR POSTURE: CAUSES AND RISKS

Poor posture can be developed due to watching TV or sitting in front of the computer for long periods, wearing improper shoes, sleeping on poor mattresses, weakness of muscles, poor sleeping, sitting, and standing habits, unhealthy weight, and so on. Other factors, such as accidents, can also be responsible for poor posture. It can affect a person's well-being by giving rise to misalignment of bones, joint pain and stiffness, and muscle strain. However, it is possible to improve body posture.

SLEEPING POSTURE

Always sleep in a position that supports the curve of the back. Make sure the pillow is under the neck but not the shoulders. The pillow should not be very thick. Sleep on your back with a pillow under the lower back or a lumbar roll under the knees. Sleeping on the sides with the knees slightly bent is one of the most recommended sleeping positions.

DID YOU KNOW?

- It's important to be aware of your posture when you're on the phone. Leaning the head and neck to one side or cradling the phone between the head and shoulders increases the chances of neck pain and stiffness.
- The proper posture to stand up requires one to keep the head high and chin forward, shoulders back, stomach in, and chest out to increase balance.

NUTRITION FOR FITNESS

A healthy diet provides the energy and nourishment that keeps the body fit and healthy. A balanced diet is the one that contains all the essential nutrients such as vitamins, minerals, carbohydrates, proteins, fats, roughage, and water. The body requires all these nutrients *in sufficient amounts for the maintenance of the cells, tissues, and organs, and for supporting normal growth and development. Lack of a balanced diet can cause* malnutrition, *especially in children.*

WORDS TO UNDERSTAND

FAMISHED: extremely hungry

MALNUTRITION: a medical condition (also called malnourishment) in which the body suffers from lack of nutrients

NUTRIENTS: substances such as vitamins and minerals that are essential for growth and health

WHY DO WE NEED NUTRIENTS?

Proteins are required for growth and repair. Meats and dairy products are rich sources of protein. Carbohydrates and fats provide energy and are found in potatoes, bread, cereals, rice, and sugar. Vitamins and minerals boost the immune system and help in growth and development. Fruits and vegetables are excellent sources of vitamins and minerals. Vitamins help the body to perform the biological processes smoothly, whereas minerals are required by the body to perform the metabolic functions. Minerals also help to build bones. The body also needs a lot of water. Fruits such as watermelon, lettuce, and oranges contain large quantities of water.

WHY IS BREAKFAST IMPORTANT?

Breakfast is the most important meal of the day because the body needs energy and nutrients in the morning after eight or more hours of sleep. Hence, breakfast refuels the body for performing the routine tasks of the day ahead. Those who skip breakfast experience a drop in their energy levels as the day progresses.

Here's some more information about healthy eating.

This may force a person to feel famished and binge on high-calorie foods or end up overeating. Skipping breakfast is one of the causes of gaining weight.

HEALTHY SNACKING

Eating a well-balanced diet is the key to a healthy body. However, eating after long gaps leads one to overeat, thereby increasing the chances of unwanted weight gain. Eating small, healthy meals throughout the day is a good way of recharging your batteries and keeping your weight in check. Avoid eating fried snacks or foods prepared with unnatural substances, toxins, and artificial sweeteners. You must remember that snacks are healthy as long as you eat them in moderate quantities. Overeating must be avoided at all costs.

LUNCH AND DINNER FOR ACTIVE METABOLISM

Eating in the middle of the day, a few hours after breakfast, re-energizes your body and raises blood sugar levels to keep you going for the rest of the day. Eating lunch also keeps your metabolism active. Dinner should always be the lightest meal of the day since the body has to go to rest after the night's meal. Skipping any of these meals is not a healthy habit.

DID YOU KNOW?

- An adult needs about eight glasses of water every day; however, some of this water can come from foods such as fruit.
- Roughage or fiber helps in the process of digestion.

DRUG ABUSE

Drug abuse is a serious health problem that affects many of us in one way or another. It refers to a patterned and continued use of drugs that is not approved or supervised by medical professionals. Abusing drugs often leads to addiction (a compulsive use of drugs). Both drug abuse and addiction are chronic psychophysical diseases.

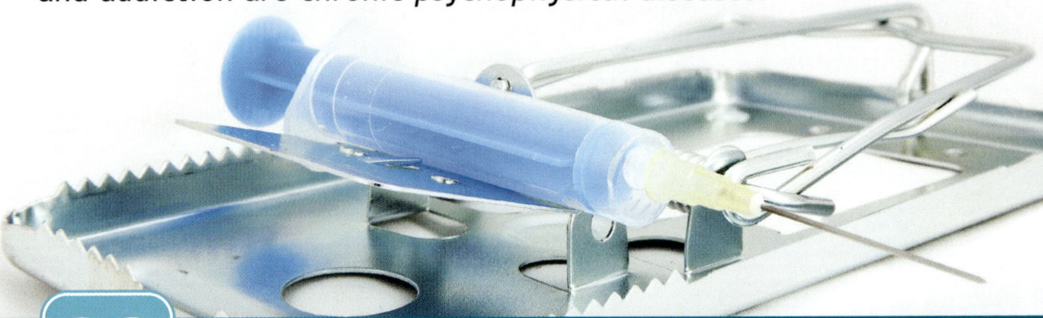

WORDS TO UNDERSTAND

CENTRAL NERVOUS SYSTEM: the brain and spinal cord; responsible for controlling all the movements of the body

CIRRHOSIS: a disease involving degeneration of liver cells

EMPHYSEMA: a serious medical condition of the lungs in which a person cannot breathe properly

FERMENTING: the chemical breakdown of a substance in which sugar is converted into carbon dioxide and alcohol with the help of yeast or other microbe

RECREATIONAL: something that is done for enjoyment

ALCOHOL

Alcohol is one of the world's oldest known drugs. It is made by fermenting grains, fruits, or vegetables. Alcohol gets absorbed into the bloodstream and affects the central nervous system. The effects of alcohol can range from something mild such as bad breath, hangover, and loss of appetite to severe conditions such as memory loss, damage to the heart and the central nervous system, cirrhosis, and liver cancer. Alcohol changes a person's perceptions, speech, movement, hearing, and vision for as long as its intoxication lasts.

TOBACCO

Tobacco is a plant grown for its leaves that are used for a variety of purposes, such as chewing, smoking, and sniffing. The tobacco leaves contain a chemical substance called nicotine, which is highly addictive. It stimulates the nervous system and produces complex neurotransmitter disruptions. Continued tobacco consumption can cause health problems such as heart disease, cancers, emphysema, and bronchitis.

PRESCRIPTION DRUG ABUSE

Taking prescription drugs in a frequency and quantity not recommended by doctors or without a medical prescription is known as prescription drug abuse. Since prescription drugs are legal, people think that there are no risks associated with them. However, their use over a long period can be dangerous to health. Three types of prescription drugs most commonly abused are opioids (painkillers), central nervous system depressants (tranquilizers and sedatives), and stimulants. They alter brain activity and can cause both addiction and physical dependence.

DRUG ADDICTION AND THE BRAIN

Every abused drug produces different physical effects, but all of them have one common impact—they alter the functioning of the brain. This has a direct impact on one's ability to feel normal without drugs. Although the initial decision to take drugs is voluntary for most people, the consequent changes in the functioning of the brain render a person completely incapable of controlling the intense urges to take drugs. Recreational drugs can increase the level of dopamine (mood-controlling hormone) in a person's brain by triggering feelings of pleasure. The brain remembers these feelings and wants them repeated.

MEDICAL HELP

Many medical treatments are available for controlling the craving for drugs. Dropping a drug addiction without the help of a doctor can be dangerous. Medical treatments are generally used along with counseling and behavioral therapy. People can also join support groups that help them associate and interact with others who understand what they are going through.

DID YOU KNOW?

- The alcohol level in blood can be checked by measuring the alcohol vapor in exhaled air with the help of a device called a "breathalyzer."
- According to the WHO, a person dies prematurely from tobacco-related diseases every 6.5 seconds.

AGING

Aging is a slow and continuous biological process of growth and development. It brings into effect changes in the whole body as the years go by. There is a steady decline in the functions of various organs and organ systems.

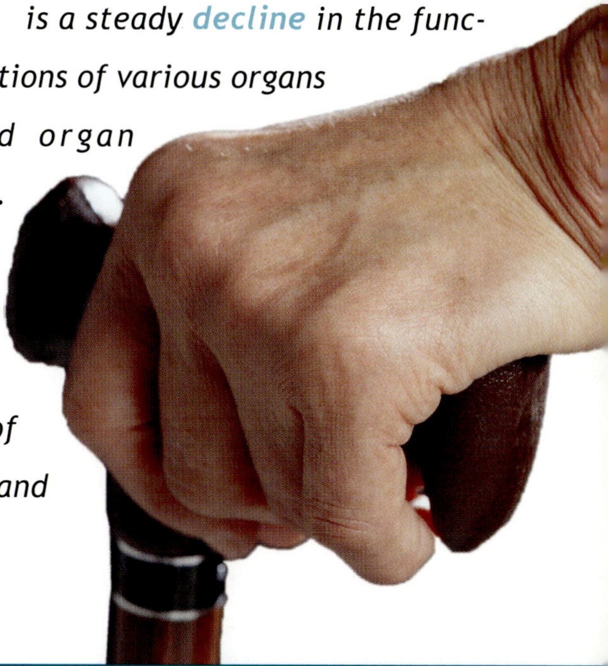

The changes that occur due to aging make a person vulnerable to various diseases and infections. Aging also increases the chances of developing medical complications and other side effects.

WORDS TO UNDERSTAND

CONTINUOUS: constant, uninterrupted

DECLINE: decay, worsening

ELASTIC: able to bend, flexible

CAUSES OF AGING

Aging occurs because the cells and tissues wear out and die over time. This leads to loss of bodily functions and increases the risk of death. Unhealthy lifestyle choices—smoking and drinking alcohol, as well as lack of physical activity—accelerate the process of aging. Hormonal imbalances, increased stress levels, anxiety, and depression can speed up the aging process. Environmental factors such as pollution also influence aging.

EFFECTS OF AGING

The body goes through many changes due to aging. Some of these changes occur outside the body while some occur inside. Over time, the skin becomes drier and less elastic, and develops wrinkles. The amount of fat stored beneath the skin decreases, which makes bones more visible. Bones and muscles become weaker and the flexibility of joints is reduced. Muscle mass, strength, and physical endurance also decrease. Age can bring memory lapses as well as loss of coordination and balance. The immune system becomes weaker and loses its efficiency to guard against infections.

SLOWING THE PROCESS

Though aging is unavoidable, you can slow down its pace. A healthy lifestyle, balanced diet, regular exercise, and drinking lots of water help slow down aging. The body responds to any form of physical activity regardless of age, which means that people as young as

5 years or as old as 70 can reap the benefits of physical activities. According to many medical studies, people over the age of 65 need to be fit to be independent, recover from illness, as well as to reduce the risk of diseases and infections.

OLDER PEOPLE SHOULD EXERCISE

Some people think that older people should not exercise. There is also a fear that they might end up injuring themselves during workouts. This is not necessarily true. Older people should engage in light exercise to keep their body systems working properly. Exercising is good for both physical and mental health. Muscle strength, which is essential in old age, can decrease due to lack of exercise.

DID YOU KNOW?

- According to the National Council on Aging, about 80 percent of older adults have one or more chronic diseases.
- About 7 million older Americans struggle with depression.

MYTHS AND FACTS

Sometimes people pass on "information" that is actually a **myth***, without any* **evidence***. There are many myths related to health and fitness that are believed to be true. Unfortunately, many people fashion their diet and exercise regimen keeping such myths in mind. It is advisable to double-check before accepting fitness and diet advice.*

WORDS TO UNDERSTAND

EVIDENCE: facts that support a particular argument

MYTH: misconception

REDUCTION: lowering; trimming

YOU MUST DRINK EIGHT GLASSES OF WATER PER DAY TO BE HEALTHY.

Fact: Drinking water is important as it replaces the amount of water a person loses throughout the day. However, part of the oft-repeated "eight glasses" can come from food; for instance, fruit is an excellent source of water.

SPOT REDUCTION IS POSSIBLE.

Fact: It is not possible to trim down only a particular part of the body. Selecting an exercise routine to burn off fat from a particular area will not make one lose that excess fat. It's best to consult a professional trainer on the type of exercises one should be doing.

NO PAIN, NO GAIN.

Fact: Many people assume that exercise must hurt to be beneficial, when in fact exercising too much can cause muscle ache, muscle cramps, or spasms, as well as pain in the joints. A sensible exercise program might be uncomfortable but should not be painful. It should put a reasonable demand on the cardiorespiratory and musculoskeletal systems to improve their function without increasing the risk of injury.

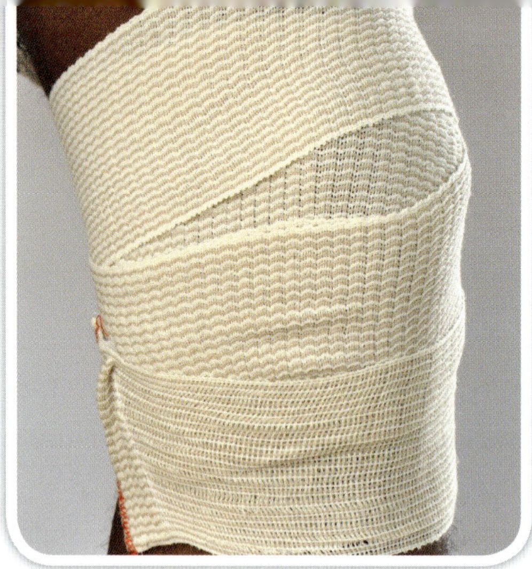

THE BEST TIME TO EXERCISE IS EARLY IN THE MORNING.

There is no particular time considered best to exercise. The time that fits into your schedule is the best time for you. Some people love to jump-start their day with a morning workout, while others think that exercising after the workday is over is a great way to energize for the evening and eliminate stress.

IF YOU EXERCISE, YOU CAN EAT WHATEVER YOU WANT.

A balanced nutrition program goes hand in hand with a sound exercise regimen. If the goal is to lose weight or maintain a healthy weight, you should add more fruits and vegetables to your diet, avoiding processed high-sugar foods and controlling portion size. A well-balanced diet along with regular exercise is still the safest and most effective way to achieve weight loss or performance goals.

HEAT MAKES INJURIES FEEL BETTER, HEAL FASTER.

Sports injuries—a sore knee, a twisted ankle, an aching elbow—hurt because of internal bleeding and swelling, very often caused by overuse. You should use ice, not heat, to reduce pain and swelling. Always have a doctor check the injury so that you can be sure that it is healing.

DID YOU KNOW?

- Running on a treadmill puts stress on our knees, just like running on asphalt.
- Working out is not only good for your body, but it improves your brain function as well.

TEXT-DEPENDENT QUESTIONS

- How does the World Health Organization define health?
- How many times does an adult's heart beat per day?
- What are some examples of anxiety disorders?
- What are some tips to reduce stress?
- What causes obesity?
- What does BMI stand for?
- Why is stretching important?
- Why use an exercise ball?
- Why is good posture important?
- What are some of the physical effects of aging?

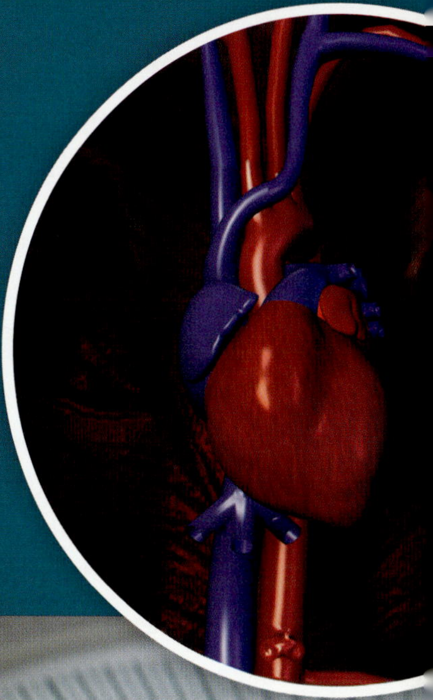

RESEARCH PROJECTS

- Using this book and online resources, develop a list of tips for people who want to start a new exercise program. What should they do? What should they not do? Turn the advice into a poster or pamphlet that people can use to get started on a new exercise program.
- Find out more about aerobic and anaerobic exercises. Try one of each and take notes about how you feel during and after the exercise. Which one did you like best and why?
- Keep a sleep diary for one week. Write down what you were doing right before bedtime, any snacks you might have eaten before going to bed, roughly how long it took you to fall asleep (as best you can remember), how many times you woke up during the night, what time you woke up, and how difficult it was to wake up. After a week, look back at your sleep habits. Are there any changes you'd like to make in order to sleep better?
- Using this source and others, find out more about fitness myths. Choose a fitness myth that interests you and find out why it's false. Make a poster or write a short essay about the myth: why do people believe it and how can we convince people it's not true?

SERIES GLOSSARY OF KEY TERMS

amino acid: an organic molecule that is the building block of proteins.

antibody: a protein in the blood that fights off substances the body thinks are dangerous.

antioxidant: a substance that fights against free radicals, molecules in the body that can damage other cells.

biofortification: the process of improving the nutritional value of crops through breeding or genetic modification.

calories: units of heat used to indicate the amount of energy that foods will produce in the human body.

carbohydrates: substances found in certain foods (such as bread, rice, and potatoes) that provide the body with heat and energy and are made of carbon, hydrogen, and oxygen.

carcinogen: something that causes cancer.

cardiovascular: of or relating to the heart and blood vessels.

carnivorous: meat-eating.

cholesterol: a soft, waxy substance present in all parts of the body, including the skin, muscles, liver, and intestines.

collagen: a fibrous protein that makes up much of the body's connective tissues.

deficiency: a lack of something, such as a nutrient in one's diet.

derivative: a product that is made from another source; for example, malt comes from barley, making it a barley derivative.

diabetes: a disease in which the body's ability to produce the hormone insulin is impaired.

dietary supplements: products taken orally that contain one or more ingredient (such as vitamins or amino acids) that are intended to supplement one's diet and are not considered food.

electrolytes: substances (such as sodium or calcium) that are ions in the body regulating the flow of nutrients into and waste products out of cells.

enzyme: a protein that starts or accelerates an action or process within the body.

flexible: applies to something that can be readily bent, twisted, or folded without any sign of injury.

food additive: a product added to a food to improve flavor, appearance, nutritional value, or shelf life.

genetically modified organism (GMO): a plant or animal that has had its genetic material altered to create new characteristics.

growth hormone: a substance either naturally produced by the body or synthetically made that stimulates growth in animals or plants.

herbicide: a substance designed to kill unwanted plants, such as weeds.

hydration: to supply with ample fluid or moisture.

macronutrients: nutrients required in large amounts for the health of living organisms, including proteins, fats, and carbohydrates.

metabolism: the chemical process by which living cells produce energy.

micronutrients: nutrients required in very small amounts for the health of living organisms.

nutritional profile: the nutritional makeup of given foods, including the balance of vitamins, minerals, proteins, fats, and other components.

obesity: a condition in which excess body fat has amassed to the point where it causes ill-health effects.

pasteurization: a process that kills microorganisms, making certain foods and drinks safer to consume.

pesticide: a substance designed to kill insects or other organisms that can cause damage to plants or animals.

processed food: food that has been refined before resale, often with additional fats, sugars, sodium, and other additives.

protein: a nutrient found in food (as in meat, milk, eggs, and beans) that is made up of many amino acids joined together, is a necessary part of the diet, and is essential for normal cell structure and function.

protein complementation: the dietary practice of combining different plant-based foods to get all of the essential amino acids.

refined: when referring to grains or flours, describing those that have been processed to remove elements of the whole grain.

sustainable: a practice that can be successfully maintained over a long period of time.

vegan: a person who does not eat meat, poultry, fish, dairy, or other products sourced from animals.

vegetarian: a person who does not eat meat, poultry, or fish.

whole grain: grains that have been minimally processed and contain all three main parts of the grain—the bran, the germ, and the endosperm.

workout: a practice or exercise to test or improve one's fitness for athletic competition, ability, or performance.

FURTHER READING

FREDERICK, SHANE. *Stamina Training for Teen Athletes. Sports Illustrated Kids*. **North Mankato, MN:** Capstone, 2012.

KENNEY, KAREN L. *Strength Training for Teen Athletes. Sports Illustrated Kids*. **North Mankato, MN:** Capstone, 2012.

NEWBY, P.K. *Food and Nutrition: What Everybody Needs to Know*. New York: Oxford University Press, 2018.

WILLIAMS, MELVIN H., J. DAVID BRANCH, AND ERIC S. RAWSON. *Nutrition for Health, Fitness, and Sport*. **New York:** McGraw Hill, 2016.

INTERNET RESOURCES

5 WAYS TO HELP UNFIT TEENS GET MOVING

Practical tips from WebMD about how to add more activity into a teenager's day.

https://www.webmd.com/parenting/raising-fit-kids/move/get-teens-moving#1

NUTRITION AND FITNESS

A thorough overview of health topics relating to eating and exercise from the Nemours Foundation.

http://kidshealth.org/en/kids/nutrition/

SAFETEENS: EXERCISE AND FITNESS

Lots of good information about getting and staying healthy.

http://www.safeteens.org/nutrition-exercise/exercise-fitness/

WELLNESS

Teen Vogue collects its articles about all aspects of wellness, from fitness and diet to self-care and mental health.

https://www.teenvogue.com/wellness/

INDEX

Photo Credits

Photographs sourced by Macaw Media, except for the following:
Cover and p. 1: © Monkey Business Images | Shutterstock; © AlenKadr | Shutterstock; © Africa Studio | Shutterstock; © Julialototskaya | Dreamstime © Gaid Phitthayakormsilp | Dreamstime; © Khatuna Bandzeladze | Dreamstime, p. 2: © pathdoc | Shutterstock, p. 3: © Africa Studio | Shutterstock ©By Oleksiy Mark | Shutterstock; ©By al7 | Shutterstock; © Vladyslav Starozhylov | Shutterstock; © zebrik | Shutterstock, p. 5: © AlenKadr Shutterstock, p. 6: © Luis Molinero | Shutterstock, p. 7: © Lotus_studio | Shutterstock, p. 8: © Ivonne Wierink | Shutterstock, p. 10: © pathdoc Shutterstock, p. 12: © Amelia Fox | Shutterstock, p. 14: © Roman Samborsky | Shutterstock, p. 15: © y V.S.Anandhakrishnr | Shutterstock, p. 17 © Hongqi Zhang | Dreamstime, p. 22: © Vaeenma | Dreamstime, p. 23: © Maya Kruchankova | Dreamstime, p. 24: © Katerynakon | Dreamstime p. 26: © Alberto Jorrin Rodriguez | Dreamstime, p. 27: © Macrovector | Dreamstime, p. 28: © Alila07 | Dreamstime, p. 30: © Iakov Filimonov Dreamstime, p. 31: © Lightfieldstudiosprod | Dreamstime, p. 32: © Konstantin Kamenetskiy | Dreamstime, p. 33: © Redbaron | Dreamstime, p. 34 © Lzf | Dreamstime, p. 35: © Antoniodiaz | Dreamstime, p. 36: © Gaid Phitthayakormsilp | Dreamstime, p. 39: © Monkey Business | Shutterstock, p 42: © Romastudio | Dreamstime, p. 43: © Irina V | Dreamstime; © Julia Gerasina | Dreamstime, p. 44: © Pixattitude | Dreamstime, p. 46: © Atstock Productions | Shutterstock, p. 47: © Syda Productions | Dreamstime, p. 51: © Pojoslaw | Dreamstime, p. 52: © Yuliya Stankevych | Dreamstime; © Khatuna Bandzeladze | Dreamstime, p. 53: © Andor Bujdoso | Dreamstime, p. 54: © Rosshelen | Dreamstime, p. 55: © Piksel | Dreamstime, p. 56: © Studioloco | Dreamstime, p. 57: © Diego Vito Cervo | Dreamstime, p. 58: ©By Valentyn Volkov | Shutterstock, p. 59: ©By Olga Miltsova | Shutterstock © By Serg64 | Shutterstock, p. 61: © Elenafetisova | Dreamstime, p. 62: © Mikkolem | Dreamstime; © Thidarat Petprasom | Dreamstime, p. 63: © Ocusfocus | Dreamstime, p. 65: © Subbotina | Dreamstime, p. 66: © Wavebreakmedia Ltd | Dreamstime, p. 69: © Luchschen | Dreamstime, p. 70: © Czuber | Dreamstime, p. 71: © Mario Kelichhaus | Dreamstime, p. 73: © Dmitrijs Mihejevs | Dreamstime, p. 75: © Yuliya Stankevych | Dreamstime p. 76: © Vitalinko | Dreamstime, p. 77: © Vitalinko | Dreamstime